fantasy

Stir this enchanted

...moon that cannot rise, and the ...ice who will do anything for his grumpy princess.

Every spell-binding story in this collection as been carefully chosen and tried out by hildren's book expert Pat Thomson. They ...re all by top children's authors from around he world, including Astrid Lindgren, Kevin Crossley-Holland and Adèle Geras.

Pat Thomson is a well-known author and anthologist of children's stories. She also works with teachers as a lecturer and librarian. She is an Honorary Vice-President f the Federation of Children's Book Groups. he is married, has two grown-up children nd lives in Northamptonshire.

A Cauldron of Magical Stories

Collected by Pat Thomson

Illustrated by Peter Bailey

CORGI BOOKS

A CAULDRON OF MAGICAL STORIES
A CORGI BOOK : 0 552 545457

PRINTING HISTORY
Corgi edition published 2000

1 3 5 7 9 10 8 6 4 2

Collection copyright © Pat Thomson, 2000
Illustrations copyright © Peter Bailey, 2000
Cover illustration by Christopher Gunson

Set in 16/20pt Bembo Schoolbook by
Phoenix Typesetting, Ilkley, West Yorkshire

Corgi Books are published by Transworld Publishers,
61–63 Uxbridge Road, London W5 5SA,
a division of The Random House Group Ltd,
in Australia by Random House Australia (Pty) Ltd,
20 Alfred Street, Milsons Point, Sydney, NSW 2061, Australia,
in New Zealand by Random House New Zealand Ltd,
18 Poland Road, Glenfield, Auckland 10, New Zealand
and in South Africa by Random House (Pty) Ltd,
Endulini, 5a Jubilee Road, Parktown 2193, South Africa

Printed and bound in Great Britain by
Cox & Wyman Ltd, Reading Berkshire

Acknowledgements

The editor and publisher are grateful for permission to include the following copyright stories:

Leila Berg, 'The Little Blue Caps', from *Folk Tales* (Brockhampton, 1966). Reprinted by kind permission of Leila Berg and the Lisa Eveleigh Literary Agency.

Kevin Crossley-Holland, 'The Dead Moon', from *The Dead Moon and other Tales from East Anglia and the Fen Country* (Andre Deutsch, 1982). Reprinted by permission of Scholastic Children's Books.

Dorothy Edwards, 'Witch at Home', from *Mists and Magic* (Lutterworth, 1983). Reprinted by permission of Rogers, Coleridge & White Ltd.

Wendy Eyton, 'The Witch at the Window', from *The Screaming Field* (Harper Collins, 1993). Reprinted by permission of the author.

Adèle Geras, 'Something More', from *Beauty and the Beast and other stories* (Hamish Hamilton, 1996). Reprinted by permission of Hamish Hamilton, © Adèle Geras 1996.

Contents

Léonie and the Last Wolf

'I'm just going to play outside,' Léonie called to her childminder.

'All right, dear, but wrap up warm,' Mrs Collins called back. She was busy giving Léonie's little twin brothers their tea.

Léonie pulled on her thick red anorak and her gloves. She put on her red boots too and then picked up a basket she had been hiding in the hall. She wasn't going out to play at all. She was going to visit her grandmother.

Granny Maple lived a bus ride away

on the other side of town and she wasn't well. Léonie had heard her parents talking about it at breakfast and she knew they were worried. Back and forth they had talked over Léonie's head, while they packed their bags for work, spooned cereal into the babies and loaded all the children into their car to go to Mrs Collins.

No-one asked Léonie what she thought about it, although she was seven, so she had grabbed a little basket, filled it with what she could and hidden it under her anorak.

Now, standing at the bus stop, she wondered if she had brought the right sort of things for a sick granny. One packet of Liquorice Allsorts, two satsumas, a comic and a carton of milk didn't look much in her basket. Léonie shivered, in spite of her warm anorak and hood. It was lonely at the bus stop and it was a very cold afternoon. A few flakes of snow drifted down.

Léonie decided to walk to the high street, where there were more people and a choice of two buses to Granny's. She knew all about getting there and had even brought her purse. Walking fast to keep warm, Léonie realized she would have to pass the end of Lupus Alley. She had always been a bit scared of its dark entrance and as she approached it, she quickened her step even more. Just as she drew level with its shadowy opening, a large grey dog slunk out of it and barred her way.

Léonie was a brave girl but she was scared of big dogs. He was enormous, with big white teeth and a lolling red tongue. He looked just like a wolf. And then, he spoke.

'Where are you going to all alone, little girl?'

'To see my grandmother, who is not well,' replied Léonie, and as she said it, realized that it was not a wise thing to say to a talking wolf.

But instead of saying, 'And where does your grandmother live?' the animal said, 'But you shouldn't be out on your own at your age. It is very dangerous. Do your parents know?'

'No,' said Léonie, 'but I know the way.'

The animal looked at her with its big amber eyes and said, 'I will come with you if you like and look after you.'

Léonie looked at him doubtfully. 'But aren't you a wolf?'

He sighed. '*The* wolf. The last one in England. Are you scared of me?'

'No,' said Léonie, because she wasn't any more. 'Should I be?'

'Of course not,' said the wolf. 'I won't hurt you.'

'But why are you the last wolf?

What happened to the others?'

'They were all killed. Hunted, shot, trapped, poisoned,' said the wolf, looking sadly down his long nose.

'But that's terrible,' cried Léonie, and she put her arm round the wolf 's neck.

'You are very unusual,' he said, nuzzling her face. 'Most people are scared of wolves.'

Léonie looked at her new friend. 'I don't think they'll let you on the bus,' she said.

'Then let's walk,' said the wolf. 'You lead the way and I'll follow at your heels. People will think I'm just your big dog.'

So Léonie and the wolf set off down the road to the high street. It was getting dark and the street lamps were coming on. As Léonie came to a side street, two big boys on skateboards nearly crashed into her. But the wolf leapt in front of

her and stood with his hackles up and
his teeth bared. The skateboarders
goggled at him, swerved and fell off.
Then they picked up their boards and
ran.

'You see what I mean?' said the wolf.
'You are too small to be out alone.'

Léonie was glad to get to the brightly
lit town centre. But there were other
dangers here. Cars drove too fast,
honking and screeching round corners.
Léonie knew her Green Cross Code but
some of the drivers didn't bother to
signal. The wolf stopped her from
stepping into the path of several turning
cars.

At the last crossing before Granny
Maple's block, Léonie waited patiently
for the lights to change. The snow was
falling thickly now and it was quite
dark, but Léonie felt warm from the
walk and safe with all the people at the

crossing and her own personal wolf. Suddenly there was a snarl and a yelp. The wolf had dashed round Léonie and now held in his jaws the hand of a man who was trying to take Léonie's purse from her basket. The other people at the lights realized what was going on.

'Fancy taking a little girl's money! Ought to be ashamed of himself!'

The wolf opened his mouth and the thief disappeared quickly into the snow, holding his wrist.

'Good guard dog you've got there,' said an old lady, patting the wolf approvingly.

Léonie stuffed the purse into her anorak pocket. 'Not far now,' she whispered to the wolf.

Granny Maple's house was right on the main road. It was rather shabby, with the paint peeling off the door and windows. Before she rang the bell,

Léonie flung both her arms round the wolf's neck and buried her face in his yellow-grey fur. It was wet with melting snowflakes and smelled of forests.

'You are the best wolf in England,' said Léonie. 'Even if you are the last.'

The wolf gently licked the salty tears from the corners of her eyes.

'I must go now, Léonie. I know how the story of the grandmother and the little girl and the wolf ends. Since I *am* the last wolf, I must be careful.'

Just then the door opened and a wedge of lemon-coloured light fell on the path. There in the doorway was Léonie's father. He snatched her up in his arms, kissing her and telling her off at the same time.

'Oh, you naughty girl! We've been so worried about you!'

The wolf slipped out of the light and over the broken wall like a shadow in

the snow. Before her father closed the door, Léonie could feel that the wolf had gone.

While Dad went to phone Léonie's mum, she crept up the stairs and into Granny's bedroom. Granny wasn't lying in bed in a nightgown and frilly nightcap. She was packing a suitcase and wearing her warm winter coat. She hugged Léonie and told her that she was coming to stay with them.

'Yes,' said Dad, appearing in the doorway, 'we think Granny is getting too old to be on her own. It's too dangerous.'

Granny made a little face that only Léonie could see. Léonie thought about how *she* was too *young* to be on her own, and wished that Granny Maple could have met the wolf.

Dad carried Granny's cases to the car and Léonie and Granny sat inside, eating Liquorice Allsorts, while Dad cleaned the snow off the windscreen. Léonie rubbed a dark circle on her window. Granny's little house looked sad to be left on its own. Then Granny said, 'Look at that beautiful dog.'

Léonie looked out through her peephole and saw her wolf for the last time. 'Can't stand that kind myself,' said her father cheerfully, getting in and starting the car. 'They always look too much like wolves for me.'

Granny turned round to smile at Léonie and winked.

This story is by Mary Hoffman.

The Lost Footbridge

Down in the little village close to the
edge of the forest, where the old
schoolmaster had recently died, a new
teacher arrived to take over the school.
He was a young man who was very
fond of children and he was always full
of kindness and understanding. The only
thing he got cross about was
unpunctuality. He could get quite angry
if a child arrived late for school. Some of
the boys and girls lived on isolated
farmsteads and had to travel a very long
way to school, but they all tried to
please him and were hardly ever late.

One winter morning, when snow and ice were thick on the ground, one little girl arrived rather late. Instead of scowling, the teacher said to her, 'Well, Jenny, I know you have a long way to come and I dare say it is not easy for you in this weather, but perhaps you could start out a little earlier tomorrow morning.'

'Oh, I did set off early enough, sir,' she replied, 'but then I remembered that I had not put out any food for our hobgoblin and I had to go back and do it. I couldn't very well leave him without food on a cold day like this, could I?'

When the teacher heard this he was very cross indeed. He thumped on the table with his fist as he said, 'What nonsense! There are no such things as goblins, elves or gremlins. Nobody has ever seen a fairy or a goblin! Such stories are just rubbish, invented by silly

21

children like you. The sooner you come to your senses the better.'

'But, sir, I have seen our hobgoblin,' cried Jenny. 'I once saw him sitting on a wooden beam high up in the barn. He was wearing a little cap and playing a tune, using a straw as a pipe. Grandmother told me that he was a real hobgoblin and that there is one in nearly every home.'

'Nonsense!' said the teacher. 'What you saw sitting on that beam was probably just your tabby cat. You can take it from me, there are no such things as hobgoblins.'

But then some of the other children spoke up and said that they had their own hobgoblin at home and they too gave him food every day. Having hobgoblins was very lucky, they said. You had to be kind to them, otherwise they would leave the house.

The teacher clapped his hands over his ears and cried. 'That is enough now! I'll have no more of it, do you hear? You are all talking a lot of nonsense. I forbid you to put out plates of food every day. As like as not, your cat will eat it the minute you turn your back, anyway.'

The children did not dare answer back; they knew in their own hearts that the teacher was wrong. But he went to all the houses in the village in turn and gave the farmers and their wives a good talking-to. It was time the children stopped this nonsense, he said, and he could not understand why they had not told them so long ago.

But the farmers did not agree with him. 'Why should we stop putting out food?' they asked. 'Hobgoblins bring luck and look after the house and home; they keep an eye on our cattle and make sure our barns don't catch fire. And a little bowl full of gruel once a day is not too much to pay for that. If we do not feed them they will move on to some other place.'

But the teacher persisted and, by and by, the children began to forget their hobgoblins. Many a day went by when no food was put out for them. As a result fewer and fewer of the goblins were to be seen about the local farmsteads.

Jenny was the only child who never forgot to feed her little friend. Every day she put out a small bowl full of gruel for him, and during the summer months she always added a little fruit – some wild strawberries, cherries or bilberries. Later on, in the autumn, she added blackberries; and, towards Christmas, a hazelnut or two.

The months went by and soon it was springtime once again. Easter came and Jenny chose her prettiest Easter egg to give to the little hobgoblin. But as she went up the stairs to the attic she was amazed to see her small friend sitting on the topmost step, resting his chin on his hands, with the pointed tip of his little red cap dangling sadly over his right eye.

'Oh, you dear little goblin,' she cried. 'At last I can see you properly! I have always wanted to talk to you.'

'Jenny, my dear, I have come to say goodbye to you,' came the sad reply. 'We hobgoblins have decided to leave the village altogether – nobody seems to want us any more. And, what is more, we shall never return!'

Jenny begged him to change his mind. He could surely stay with her, especially since she had always looked after him so well.

But he would have none of it. 'Even if I wanted to stay,' he said, 'I could not do it. As we can no longer use the magic plank I would never be able to visit my old friends, and I would be miserable without them.'

'What magic plank?' cried Jenny, 'I have never heard of a magic plank. Where is it and what has happened to it?'

'You know it all right,' said the goblin. 'Every village has one. Yours was in the little footbridge which you cross every day on your way to school. But your teacher has finally persuaded the parish council that the villagers need a brand-new footbridge, built of concrete and with an iron handrail. *We* could never use such a bridge – it just would not be right. And that is why we have to leave the village.

'Thank you for all you have done for me. I am just as sorry as you are that I should have to go from here.'

Jenny was almost in tears, but she remembered to give him the Easter egg, as a souvenir.

The little goblin was overjoyed. He had never before been given such a lovely present. He hardly knew how to thank her.

'I tell you what,' he said, 'I will give you a present before I go. I shall leave you the magic plank. I am not sure yet where I shall hide it, but you will find it sooner or later. And if you are ever in need you can walk across it and step right into our kingdom. Once you are there all will be well and I shall be delighted to see you again.'

And, before Jenny could ask any more questions, he had disappeared and so had the Easter egg.

All day long Jenny thought about the little man. When bedtime came she was still wondering where he had gone.

At about midnight she awoke from her sleep. At first, she did not know what had disturbed her, but she soon realized that it must have been the strange noise which seemed to be coming from the other side of the big barn. She climbed out of bed and went over to the window, but she could see nothing. Then she crept downstairs and went across the yard into the barn. Everything was quiet and peaceful; silver moonlight filtered through the small windows and shone through the cracks in the roof and walls.

Jenny climbed onto some bales of straw and looked out of a window to see if there was anyone behind the barn; but everything was calm and undisturbed. The apple trees stood silent in the moonlight and, further away, at the far end of the orchard she could see the cherry trees, cloaked in pink and white blossoms.

Then she heard the strange noise again: a faint thumping and bumping, a rumpling and crumpling and a tapping of tiny feet. At last she saw them! There they were, right beneath her in the long grass. Hobgoblins everywhere! They were coming from all sides, carrying bundles and boxes; some of them even stumbled under their load.

None of them seemed to know exactly where they were going until suddenly Jenny heard the sound of music. Someone was playing a sad little melody on a reed-pipe and this seemed to be their signal. The little men formed a long line and marched one after the other along the narrow path which the cats had trodden on their daily search for mice. Out into the meadow they went, and from there into the field beyond.

By and by, the patch of grass beneath

the window became quiet again. The
last of the hobgoblins had disappeared
among the dark shadows underneath
the apple trees. Jenny could no longer
see them but she could still hear the
sound of the reed-pipe for a long time
afterwards. It grew fainter and fainter
and, just as the moon began to hide her
face behind a cloud, the music stopped
altogether.

Jenny stood and waited for a little
while longer, but all she could hear was
the wind rustling through the nearby
forest. Sadly, she turned away and went
back to bed.

When she awoke the following
morning, she smiled a little at the
thought of the strange dream she had
had during the night and she was
careful to put out a small bowl of gruel
for her little hobgoblin, just as she had
always done. Only at tea-time, when she

discovered that the food had not been
touched, did she realize that the little
men had really and truly left the village.
She was very sad and downhearted.
After this, she often thought she could
still hear the sound of the reed-pipe,
especially at dusk or on moonlit nights.

Weeks and months and years rolled over
the land and Jenny grew into a young
woman. She married and had children
of her own and, by and by, she grew old
and became a grandmother. She often
told her children, and later her
grandchildren, about the hobgoblins and
the magic plank. And they often
searched for it, but no-one ever found it
– no doubt it had been chopped up for
firewood long ago. After all, lots of pieces
of timber lie about in a farmyard and
you can hardly expect a farmhand to be
able to spot a magic one, especially if his

mistress is in a hurry and needs some kindling for the kitchen stove.

Then, one sunny Easter Day, it happened: Grandmother Jenny and the children went out into the garden to search for Easter eggs. Spring flowers were in bloom everywhere. The children searched among the violets and primroses, and among the purple and yellow crocuses.

The smallest child even ventured into the barn. Among the hay and straw he found the biggest Easter egg of all. It was bright green and on it was painted the picture of a hobgoblin, wearing a tiny red cap on his head.

'My goblin! That is a picture of my very own hobgoblin,' laughed his grandmother. 'I would recognize my hobgoblin anywhere.'

All the other children ran into the barn, hoping that they too would find

such a wonderful egg. They crawled
about in the hay and straw, but all they
discovered was a wooden plank,
crumbling with age.

As soon as Grandmother Jenny saw it
she knew that this must be the magic
plank she had been searching for all
these years. And what was this? Surely
she could hear the sound of a reed-pipe
playing that melancholy tune of long
ago?

She asked the children to lay the
plank across the little brook which ran
along the bottom of the orchard, where
the buttercups stood thick and golden
like a carpet.

Grandmother Jenny listened again.
'Yes,' she said, 'I can hear my friends
calling me from the distance. Can you
hear their sweet music, my little ones?
Let me kiss you goodbye, for I must go
to them.'

She gave each one of the children a hug and a kiss and then she stepped carefully across the plank and walked through the meadow on the other side into the forest.

The boys and girls watched her until she disappeared among the tall pine trees. Suddenly, they too could hear faint music, but when they wanted to follow their grandmother they found that the old plank had turned to dust and was no more than a brown patch amongst the yellow flowers on the banks of the brook.

This story is by Wilhelm Matthiessen.

Prince Amilec

In a palace by the sea lived a beautiful princess. She had eyes as green as apples, long red hair, and a very nasty temper indeed.

One day, her father said that she should think about getting married. Lots of princes had thought they would like to marry her in the past, but once she had flown into a rage with them a few times, they changed their minds and went off to find someone a bit quieter.

'I don't want to get married,' said the princess. 'And I *won't*!' And she picked up a china dog to throw at her father.

He dodged out of the room, just in time.

'I'm getting too old for all this running about,' he said to his secretary. 'I really must get her married off, and then her husband can deal with her.'

'Don't worry,' said the secretary. 'I'll get some messengers to ride around the other kingdoms with the princess's portrait. A lot of people will be interested, and they won't know till they get here what she's like.'

Now, in one of the kingdoms that the messenger visited there lived a handsome young prince named Amilec. When the portrait was brought in, the prince immediately fell in love with the princess in the picture. No sooner were the messengers out of the room than Amilec grabbed his cloak and was riding full speed up the road toward the sea.

When he reached the palace, he found a good many suitors there already. They were waiting for a glimpse of the princess, who was supposed to appear at one of the palace windows and graciously wave to them.

Suddenly a window shot up and a red head appeared.

'Go *away*!' bawled the princess, and went in again.

'Ha, ha!' cried the king, who was leaning anxiously out of another window. 'She will have her little joke!'

The suitors laughed uneasily, and the butler came and showed them to their rooms.

'My dear,' said the king cautiously, 'couldn't you just try? All those nice young men have come such a long way.'

'Don't worry,' said the princess. 'I'll soon get rid of them. I'm going to set them such impossible tasks that they'll give up and go home inside a week.'

Sure enough, when all the suitors had gathered in the dining room, the princess's page came down, asked for silence, and took out a scroll.

'The princess,' read the page, 'wishes to inform you that she has thrown her ruby bracelet out the tower window into the sea. Before any of you think of asking for her hand, you must dive down and get it back for her.'

None of the suitors felt like eating their dinner after that. Some went out immediately and began to pack their bags; others flew into a rage and banged their fists on the table. Prince Amilec put his head in his hands and groaned. The page felt rather sorry for Amilec, who was the only suitor who had not been rude to him.

'If I were you, I should just go home and forget about the princess,' whispered the page. 'She's frightful!'

'I can't,' said Amilec sorrowfully. 'I shall have to look for her bracelet, even if I drown in the attempt.'

'I'll tell you what, then,' said the page. 'Further up the beach lives a witch in a cave. Nobody's ever seen her, but she's supposed to be very clever. She might help you, if you asked her nicely.'

Prince Amilec wasn't too keen on visiting a witch, but he thanked the page, and went and thought about it. Eventually he decided that it was a lot safer than diving into the sea on his own.

When the palace clock struck twelve, he went quietly out and down the path to the beach. At last he came to a cave

with a big front door set in it, covered
over by a lot of seaweed. Prince Amilec
knocked, feeling rather nervous.

'The witch will probably be horribly
ugly, with three eyes and a wart on the
end of her nose,' Amilec said to himself.
'But I mustn't let her see that I'm not
completely used to people with three
eyes and warts, or she may be offended
and not help me.'

Just then the door opened, and there
stood a very pretty girl holding a
lantern.

'Can I help you?' asked the girl.

'Oh – er, yes. I was looking for the
witch,' said Amilec, brushing off the
seaweed that had fallen on him when
the door opened.

'I *am* the witch,' said the girl. 'Do
come in.'

She took him down a long cave-
corridor, and at the end was another

door. The witch hung the lantern on a hook in the wall, opened the door, and led the prince into a small cozy room, where a fire was burning on the hearth.

'I thought,' said Amilec, 'that witches were old and ugly, and lived in ruined castles full of bats.'

'Well,' said the girl, 'I do have a bat.' She pointed and Amilec saw a furry shape with folded wings hanging upside down in an armchair on the other side of the fire.

'Do sit down,' said the witch. 'I'll just hang Basil on the mantelpiece.' Which she did. 'Now tell me what the trouble is.'

So Amilec told her about the red-haired princess, and how he wanted very much to marry her, and about the ruby bracelet that he had to try to find.

'I don't mind helping you,' said the witch when he had finished, 'but the princess will never marry you, you know.

And she has a dreadful temper. I can hear her down here sometimes when she starts shouting.'

Prince Amilec sighed and said he thought that might be the case but he just couldn't help being in love with the princess, however awful she was.

'All right,' said the witch. 'Leave everything to me. You just stay here and look after Basil, and see that the fire doesn't go out.'

So saying, she left the room, and a minute later Amilec heard the cave door shut. He couldn't help being curious, and as there was a small round window in the cave wall, he looked out of it to see where she had gone. The witch was walking along some rocks that ran into the sea. Suddenly she changed into a dolphin, leaped forward, and vanished in the water.

Amilec tried not to be too surprised.

He put some more wood on the fire and hung Basil a bit further along the mantelpiece, so the smoke wouldn't get into his fur.

Not long after, the cave door opened and the witch, no longer looking a bit like a dolphin, came back into the room. She held a ruby bracelet in her hand.

'Sorry I was so long,' said the witch, 'but a sea serpent had got his tail stuck in it, and I had to pull him out.'

'How can I ever thank you?' gasped Amilec.

'Don't give it a second thought,' said the witch. 'I haven't had an excuse to change into a dolphin for ages.'

Next morning, the princess called all the suitors into a big room and asked them if they had had any luck. Of course, none of them had, although some of them had been swimming about since dawn, and most of them had caught bad colds.

Just then Amilec came in. He walked up to the princess, bowed, and handed her the ruby bracelet.

'Oh!' screamed the princess. 'This can't be the right one,' she added hysterically. However, the king, who had given it to her in the first place, came up and had a look, and declared that it was.

'Well done, my boy,' he added to Amilec.

'Yes, well done,' said the princess quickly. 'Now that you've succeeded with the first task, you can go on and do the second. Everybody else is disqualified.'

So the other suitors snuffled and coughed and complained their way out, and went home.

'The second task,' said the princess, smiling a nasty smile, 'is to find my golden girdle. I have tied it to the arrow of one of the bowmen, and when he fires, goodness only knows where it will end up.'

'Perhaps I could tell him where to aim,' whispered the king's secretary.

'Certainly not!' cried the princess, who had overheard, and she went to the window and gave a signal to the bowman.

When Prince Amilec went out to look for the golden girdle, he found that there was a forest growing at the back of the palace, full of thick fern. He searched till dusk, and then he sat down on a stone, because he was worn out.

'I'll never find it,' he said. 'I might just as well go home right now.'

Just then a figure came through the

forest toward him, carrying a lantern and a bat.

'Hello,' said the witch. 'I've just been taking Basil for a fly. You look unhappy. Is it that princess again?'

'I'm afraid it is,' said Amilec.

'I thought so,' said the witch. 'What does she want now?'

Amilec told her about the golden girdle which had been fired into the forest.

'Oh, that's easy,' said the witch. 'Hold Basil, and I'll see what I can do.'

So Amilec sat on the stone with the lantern and Basil. One by one the stars came out, and the sea sounded very drowsy, as if it were going to sleep. Prince Amilec closed his eyes and dreamed that he had won the hand of the red-haired princess and she had just thrown her crown at him. He woke up with a start and found an owl sitting on the ground, a golden girdle in its beak.

'Here we are,' said the owl, changing back into the witch. 'Sorry I was so long, but some doves had got it tangled up in their nest and I had to get it out and put the nest back for them afterward.'

'How can I ever repay you?' implored Amilec.

'Come and have a cup of tea with me,' said the witch. So he did.

The next morning the princess called him into the big room and sneered at him.

'There's no need to say anything,' said the princess. 'Just pack your things and go home. Of course, if you'd care to send me a golden girdle to replace the old one, I might give you a kiss.'

Prince Amilec took out the girdle

and handed it to her.

The princess screamed, 'I don't believe it! It's not mine – it isn't!'

'Oh, yes, it is,' said the king. 'Well done, my boy.'

'Yes,' said the princess. 'Well done. You can now go on to the third task.'

Amilec paled.

'You see this pearl necklace,' said the princess with a ghastly smile. 'On it are one hundred and fifty pearls.'

The king realized what was coming and tried to stop her, but it was too late. The princess tugged on the silver chain and it broke, and the pearls flew everywhere.

'I want you to find them all, and return them to me in one hour's time.' And she glided out.

'We can help,' cried the king and the secretary.

'No, you can't!' cried the princess,

rushing back. The king and the secretary hurried away.

'Now what am I to do?' Amilec wondered. He looked out the window, and who should be walking along the seashore below the palace, gathering seaweed in a basket, but the witch. The prince leaped downstairs and out through the garden gate and along the beach.

'Hello!' said Amilec. 'How's Basil?'

'Basil's very well, thank you,' replied the witch. 'How are you getting on with the princess?'

Amilec sighed deeply and told her about the pearl necklace.

'Wouldn't it be simpler to forget all about it and go home?' asked the witch.

'I'm afraid I love the princess much too much to do that,' murmured Amilec.

'All right,' said the witch. 'You collect me some seaweed in the basket, and I'll

go and do what I can.' And she changed
into a mouse and ran through the
palace gate.

About half an hour later, the witch
came back and handed Amilec a
velvet bag.

'You said one hundred and fifty
pearls, but I found one hundred and
fifty-one, so your princess can't count.'

'Here's your seaweed. I can never
thank you enough,' said Amilec.

'That's all right,' said the witch. 'Come
down and tell me what happens.'

When Prince Amilec went back into the
palace, the princess was already sitting
waiting. Amilec went forward and tipped
all the pearls into her lap.

'Count them!' shouted the princess.

The secretary hurriedly obeyed.
'One hundred and fifty-one,' he declared
at last. The princess shrieked and

fainted with fury.

'This is the happiest day of my life,' beamed the king. 'At last – you can marry her.'

Just then the princess revived.

'Very well,' she snapped. 'I'm yours, you pest, but before I marry you I want a splendid wedding dress, and if I don't like it, I shall change my mind.'

By this time Amilec was getting a bit fed up with her tantrums, but he thought that, of all her demands, this was the most reasonable. So he bowed and said that he'd do his best.

'See that you do!' yelled the princess, and flounced out.

That night the prince made his way down the path to the witch's cave and knocked. The witch let him in, hung Basil on the mantelpiece, and sat him in the armchair.

'She wants a wedding dress now,' said Amilec, as the witch put on the kettle.

'Oh, does she?' said the witch. 'Well, how would you like me to make her a special magic one?'

'You're marvellous!' said Amilec.

The witch smiled and lifted Basil down for a moment while she got out the teapot. 'I'll bring it up to the castle first thing tomorrow morning.'

'How can I ever thank you enough?' asked Amilec.

'I'll think of something,' said the witch.

The next morning the whole court gathered worriedly.

When Amilec came in, the princess jumped up and demanded, 'Where is it?'

'A friend of mine is bringing it,' said the prince. 'She'll be here any moment.'

Just then the doors opened and in

came the most beautiful girl the prince
had ever seen. The court sighed with
wonder, the secretary dropped his pen,
and even the princess forgot to be rude.

The girl came up to the prince, and
said, 'Here is the dress. I thought it would
look better with someone wearing it. It's
made of moonlight and star-glow, and
the glitter on a mermaid's tail. I hope
you like it.'

'But who are you?' gasped Amilec.

'I am the witch.'

Then, in front of the court, the king,
and the princess, Amilec bowed to the
witch and said, 'How can I ever have
been so blind! You are the most beautiful
girl I have ever met. You are also the
kindest. May I humbly ask you to be my
wife? I promise to look after Basil, and
I'll live in the cave, if it will make things
easier.'

'Dear Amilec,' said the witch. 'Basil

and I both love you very much, and will
be delighted to accept.'

So Amilec and the witch got married
and lived happily ever after with Basil,
although Basil was asleep most of the
time.

As for the red-haired princess, when
she had finished shouting and
screaming, she told the king that what
she really wanted to do was travel. The
king was only too glad to see her go,
and packed her off as soon as possible.

One day, however, the princess came
to a kingdom where there was a
handsome prince, and she thought he
was just the kind of young man who
would be good enough for her. So
she went and knocked on the door of his
palace.

'Come in, my dear,' said the queen.
'How pretty you are! I should like my
son to marry someone like you. The

only trouble is, he always makes
princesses complete dreadful tasks before
he'll even look at them. The latest thing
he wants done is for somebody to make
an apple tree grow upside down from his
bedroom ceiling. However, I've heard
that there's a wizard who lives in the
wood, and he might help you, if you
asked him nicely.'

'Oh, well,' thought the princess, setting
off for the wood. 'The wizard will
probably be horribly ugly, with three
eyes, and a wart on the end of his nose,
but it can't be helped.'

This story is by Tanith Lee.

Something More . . .

One morning at dawn, a poor fisherman dragged his net to the shore and found, tangled up in it, a most beautiful fish.

'Your scales are silver and pearl,' said the fisherman. 'You are the noblest fish I have ever seen, and I must return you to deep waters.'

'I give you thanks,' said the fish. 'I am no sea creature, but an enchanted prince, and if I am the noblest of my kind, then surely you have more goodness in you than most men.'

The fisherman helped the beautiful fish to slip again into the quiet waves, and then he returned to his home.

The fisherman and his wife lived in a hovel. There were holes in the roof, the windows lacked glass, and the walls were black with smoke from the fire.

'There was something wondrous in my catch today,' said the fisherman to his wife. 'An enchanted prince in the shape of a beautiful fish. I put him back into the water and he was full of gratitude.'

'Dolt!' said the fisherman's wife. 'You could have asked a favour in return. Perhaps this fish is powerful as well as beautiful. Finish your porridge and get down to the shore and summon him.' She sighed. 'I was cursed with a fool for a husband, a man who cannot see good fortune when it sits on the end of his nose. Ask the fish for a pleasant cottage.'

The fisherman went down to the water's edge. The waves rolled over the sand, and beyond the breakers, the sea moved and murmured quietly. The fisherman said:

'Beautiful fish
come to the shore.
My wife has a wish
for something more.'

The fish rose up on the crest of the next wave and landed at the fisherman's feet. The fish said:

'Tell me what you heard her say.
I shall listen and obey.'

The fisherman hung his head.
'She would like a cottage in which to live.'
The fish plunged back into the

waters, and the fisherman made his way home, thinking, 'Well, I have asked, and even if the fish cannot work a miracle, I can do no more.'

When the fisherman arrived at the place where his hovel used to be, there was the prettiest cottage he had ever seen, with a little kitchen garden at the back of it, and a little flower garden at the front.

'Come and see!' shouted his wife from the door. 'It is exactly what I dreamed of! I even have a dresser with four and twenty plates displayed upon it! What a fine time we shall have here, beloved!'

For some days, the fisherman's wife was happy in her new home, but one day she said to her husband, 'I should have asked for a palace, while I had the chance. Get down to the sea at once, husband, and summon the beautiful fish. If he can do so much, perhaps he can do more. The grandest of all palaces is what I require.'

The fisherman went down to the water's edge. A wind blew off the water, and the clouds were grey and low. He said:

'Beautiful fish
come to the shore.
My wife has a wish
for something more.'

The fish was there before him in an instant, saying:

'Tell me what you heard her say.
I shall listen and obey.'

The fisherman blushed for shame.
'She would like a palace in which to live.'

The fish plunged back into the water

and the fisherman made his way home. His cottage had gone when he arrived and in its place was the most magnificent palace imaginable.

'How delightful this is!' cried the fisherman's wife. 'I have four and twenty bedrooms, a ballroom, a gallery, a scullery, and a table in the banqueting hall set with gold and silver dishes. What a fine time we shall have here, beloved!'

In a few days, however, the fisherman's wife began to complain again.

'A palace is of no use,' she said, 'without the power to go with it. Get down to the sea at once, husband, and summon the beautiful fish. I want to be the king.'

'Ladies are usually queens,' said the fisherman.

'Queens are not as powerful as kings,' said his wife. 'A king and only a king is what I wish to be.'

The fisherman went down to the water's edge. The sea was angry and dark, rolling and heaving from the shore to the horizon under a copper sky. The fisherman said:

'Beautiful fish
come to the shore.
My wife has a wish
for something more.'

The waves rose up and up and the fish crashed onto the sand, saying:

'Tell me what you heard her say.
I shall listen and obey.'

The fisherman stared down at his feet. 'She wants to be king.'
The fish plunged back into the water and the fisherman made his way home. There were four and twenty soldiers

standing guard outside the palace, and the rooms were full of courtiers, in rustling robes. His wife was sitting on an enormous golden throne, wearing a crown studded with rubies and emeralds the size of pigeons' eggs.

'Bow down before me,' she said to her husband, 'and kiss the hem of my gown. From now on, you must call me "Your Majesty" or I shall fling you into my deepest dungeon.'

The fisherman's wife enjoyed being king, but it was not enough for her.

'I should like,' she said to her husband, 'to be the leader of all the churches in the world, and tell everyone how to organize their prayers and ceremonies.'

The fisherman went down to the water's edge. Zigzags of lightning cut across the sky, and thunder sounded in the west. The sea was black and furious, and the waves made such a terrible noise

as they broke on the shore that the fisherman's words were almost lost:

'Beautiful fish
come to the shore.
My wife has a wish
for something more.'

The thunder was closer now, and out
of all the roaring came the words of the
fish:

'Tell me what you heard her say.
I shall listen and obey.'

The fisherman sobbed in anguish.
'She wants to be the leader of every
church in the world,' he said.

The fish plunged back into the water
and the fisherman made his way home.
The palace had disappeared, and in its
place was a cluster of buildings: a

cathedral, a mosque, and a synagogue all together. Four and twenty candles were burning; choirs were singing; every kind of person was praying every possible kind of prayer, and the fisherman's wife, dressed in purple silk, sat on an ivory throne under an enormous stained-glass window.

'Bless you, my husband,' she said. 'Kneel down and offer up a prayer of thanks.'

After some weeks, the fisherman's wife said to her husband, 'Do you see how God makes the sun rise in the east and set in the west? I should like to do that. Go down to the shore and ask the fish to make me into God.'

The fisherman went down to the water's edge. Dawn was breaking, and there was a golden silence lying over the still waters. The fisherman whispered:

'Beautiful fish
come to the shore.
My wife has a wish
for something more.

The fish slid on to the sand and said:

'Tell me what you heard her say.
I shall listen and obey.'

The fisherman began to weep.
'She wishes to be God,' he sobbed.
'She will not be satisfied with less.'
'Alas,' said the fish, 'she has asked for
too much.'
When the fisherman returned to his
home, what he saw was neither a palace
nor a cottage, but the same hovel that he
and his wife had lived in before he found
the beautiful fish. His wife was weeping,
but the fisherman thought how he
would never have to ask the beautiful

fish for anything ever again, and he smiled to himself and began to mend his nets.

This story is by Adèle Geras.

Witch at Home

'Several of the inhabitants of these parts are the descendants of witches,' said the woman in grey, waving her hand in a generous sweep that embraced all the valleys and little streams lying at our feet.

She was not at all the sort of person one expected to find upon a mountain summit on a hot afternoon. Clad in a neat suit with a black hat and handbag, and wearing medium-heeled shoes, she had the appearance of a respectable servant of the confidential sort —

a lady's maid or companion.

I had set off to climb the steep mountain path that morning. It was a hot day, and I was glad to reach the top. The woman was already there, sitting neatly on a slab of rock. I sat down beside her to get my breath back and enjoy the cool mountain breeze. We fell to discussing the peak on which we were sitting. 'Malkin's Ridge' it was called. The woman told me 'Malkin' was a traditional name for a witch, and that the mountain had been a favourite haunt of witches in olden times.

'Of course, there are drawbacks to having witches in the family,' said the woman. 'Take us, for instance. My granny was a witch and *her* granny before her. Indeed, I heard that Great-Great-Great-Granny's granny was burned by order of the Magistrates of her day. My granny had a pretty bad time with the villagers herself. They pulled down her cottage and threw her into the duckpond, which was fortunately not very full at the time.

'But that was in Queen Victoria's time, that was, and what with all the new steam engines and the electric telegraphs, by then the magistrates had given up believing in witches, so half the village was sent to prison and the other half was fined.

'The Squire's lady wife got up a subscription among the local gentry for Granny. They settled her down in a nice new little cottage with lace curtains and everything, and basins of hot soup every day, and free coals and potatoes.

'It was all clean and new to begin with, but Gran soon made herself at home. Once she had encouraged a few spiders and been out on one or two midnight trips round the local graveyards, it looked quite home-like. In fact, in six months you couldn't tell the lace curtains from the cobwebs.

'Mind you, Squire's Lady wasn't pleased. But when Gran made her up a bottle of special medicine that cured her rheumatism, she wouldn't hear a word against her. In fact, she grew quite proud of Granny – said she was "quaint" and used to bring her friends round to watch while Granny made her brews.

'Now, my gran was very respected in witch-circles. There was always a special place reserved for her at the Sabbat meetings. She had a lot to say in the running of the coven – in fact, you could say she was a sort of chairman of their committee.

'But alas, my mum was her only child, and she turned out a real disappointment. She just didn't show any interest in the witch profession at all. She hadn't the head for it, I suppose!

'Even a simple little thing like turning herself into a hare went wrong so that she couldn't get back to normal in time for school next day, and my poor granny had to keep her in a hutch beside the back door telling goodness knows what lies to school inspectors until the spell wore off of its own accord – it hadn't been a strong one, fortu-nately! The only time Mum ever mounted a broomstick she fell off and went right through the vicar's conserva-tory roof! As Granny said, the only use my mother had for a broomstick was for sweeping floors!

'Mad about housework was my mum. No-one knew where she got it from, but there it was. I remember Granny saying that as a baby she'd sit up in her crib and rub away at its wickerwork with the corner of her little blanket for all the world as if she were cleaning it – before she'd grown a tooth to her head!

'Poor Granny did her best, of course. She even engaged a very expensive continental warlock to tutor Mum in the Secret Arts, and she set her up with a fine black cat whose ancestry stretched back to ancient Egypt. But the warlock admitted after only one day's teaching that Mum's was a hopeless case, and was so sorry for Granny that he refused to take a penny of his fee. As for the black cat, after sharpening its claws once or twice on the hearth rug and getting scolded for it by my mum who couldn't bear the rasping noise, it just got up and walked out of the house, and was never seen again.

'The final blow fell when Mum was eighteen or so. Poor old Granny flew home one night after a particularly successful weekend rally of the

Northumberland Malkins to find that her bundles of herbs, her charms, the stuffed alligator and all her bottles of potions had been thrown out onto the rubbish heap.

'In her absence, Mum had given in to temptation and spring-cleaned the house! The windows were shining, the lace curtains had been resurrected, washed and starched, and now hung in all their glory with a couple of red geraniums in pots on the window-sill between them, and instead of spiders there was a nice yellow canary bird in a cage singing away happily.

'Granny saw then that she must accept the inevitable. She must just get Mother out of the place. She would have to look around for some nice young man to take her off her hands.

'What my mum needed was a good

husband and a cottage of her own where she could clean and polish and brew and bake to her heart's content.

'Mind you, it was a bitter blow to the family pride and Gran said she sobbed aloud as she carted all her little bits and pieces back indoors. And, as you know, witches are unable to shed tears so it was quite a painful experience for the dear old soul.

'It wasn't easy to find a young man willing to take my mother on – even though she was pretty as a picture and as good as gold – for although the law mightn't consider our Gran a witch, the villagers weren't taking any chances, and the young men kept away.

'At last Granny had to resort to love-charms. And with Mother grumbling all the time about the smells and the mess on the clean kitchen floor, Granny brewed enough love

potion to start off a hundred weddings.
It was so strong that the barest whiff
drifting across the village roofs below
was enough. In no time at all there
wasn't a young man left in the village.
They were all clustered around Granny's
cottage sighing and moaning and
carrying on all night, until Mother
couldn't get any sleep for the noise
outside, and threw buckets of water
out of the window over them – and even
then they only went home to change
and were back again by cockcrow!

'Naturally the village women were
furious, and no-one had so much as a
nod for my poor mother. If they
hadn't been afraid of what my granny
might have done to them, I think they
would have done Mum an injury. As it
was they sent her to coventry. She tried
to explain that she didn't fancy any of
their young men – she said it made her

feel silly to have them goggling at her
and following her around the village
every time she went for a stroll. She
asked how they would like it if, every
time they went out to shake a mat, they
stood the chance of tripping over an
exhausted suitor on the doorstep. But it
was no use. No-one was any the more
pleased with her for saying that she
didn't fancy one of their lads! Such is the
contrariness of human nature. So she
was lonely, and like all lonely people she
threw herself into her work, and as that
meant housework poor Granny had a
very uncomfortable time of it.

'I really don't know what Gran might
have attempted next, but as it happened,
things sorted themselves out very tidily.
One day they were having high words
about Mother having red-polished the
flags of the cottage path, when Squire's
Lady, new home from abroad, happened

to look in for a chat. The good lady was
amazed at the change in the appearance
of the cottage, and at the reason for the
family discord. She shook her head
reprovingly at Granny and said she was
to be congratulated upon having such a
paragon of a child. "Why," said My
Lady, "I haven't a servant in my
establishment to compare with
her. What a pity you cannot spare
her, for I should dearly love to take
her into my household."

'This was just the opportunity Granny
needed! It took her some time to
convince Squire's Lady that she really
wouldn't stand in her own girl's light
when it came to getting a grand job in a
great house, but as soon as My Lady
saw that Gran was in earnest, she said
she would take Mother into service at
once. "But," she said kindly, "I will send
her back to you on one day a week so

that she can give the place a tidy-up for you." And Gran was glad to see Mum go – even at the price of having to endure a weekly clean-out.

'When Mother got inside the Big House and saw all those rooms and corridors to clean she was delighted and set to at once to give the place a real going-over.

'After that Mum never looked back. She was in her rightful sphere. She learned to cook and darn and knit, and in due course she rose to be House-keeper to the Squire. It was then that she married my father who was Head Butler, and they stayed at the Big House until My Lady died. Then, feeling they would like to change, they decided to take on man-and-wife jobs in some of those luxury flats, and did very well indeed out of film people and rich foreigners.

'As for me, well, they got me a job in good service as soon as I left school. And I've stayed there ever since. Of course,' said the woman in grey, 'times aren't what they were.

'Yes, it was funny about my mum,' she went on, after pausing a moment to reflect, 'but Granny always said that she suspected there must have been some respectable blood in the family somewhere. There had been tales of a Second Footman, a sober young fellow, who got caught in a magic ring several generations back. It's funny how misfits happen in families!'

Finding that she had no more to say, and being now completely rested, I said, 'Well, I'll have to be going if I'm to get any tea down below.'

'Me too,' said the woman, jerking out of her reverie. 'My Lady wants me to babysit while she and His Lordship have an evening out.' She looked at her watch. 'My Goodness, I must fly,' she said.

With this, she rose to her feet. After brushing herself carefully down she reached round to the other side of the boulder on which we had been sitting, took up a broomstick which I swear I hadn't noticed until that moment and, mounting it nimbly, was soon skimming briskly downwards through the warm air.

This story is by Dorothy Edwards.

He Travels by Day and by Night

Did you listen to the radio on the
fifteenth of October last year? Did you
hear them asking for news of a boy who
had disappeared? This is what they said:

'The Stockholm police are looking for
nine-year-old Karl Anders Nilsson who
has been missing from his home at 13
North Street since 6 p.m. on the day
before yesterday. Karl Anders Nilsson
has fair hair and blue eyes and at the
time of his disappearance was wearing
brown shorts, grey pullover, and a small
red cap. Will anyone who can give

information as to his whereabouts please communicate with the police?'

That is what they said. But no information was ever given about Karl Anders Nilsson. He disappeared completely, no-one knew where. Nobody knows except me, for I am Karl Anders Nilsson.

But I do wish I could tell Ben everything. I used to play with Ben. He lives on North Street, too. His proper name is Benjamin, but everybody calls him Ben; and, of course, nobody calls me Karl Anders, they just say Andy.

I mean, they *used* to say Andy. Now that I have disappeared they can't say anything. It was only Aunt Hulda and Uncle Olaf who called me Karl Anders. Well, Uncle Olaf never really called me anything. He hardly ever spoke to me.

I was the foster child of Aunt Hulda and Uncle Olaf. I came to them when I

was a year old. Before that I lived in the
Children's Home. It was from there that
Aunt Hulda fetched me. She wanted to
adopt a girl, but there were none that
she could have. So she took me, though
Uncle Olaf and Aunt Hulda don't like
boys — not boys of eight or nine,
anyway. They thought I made too much
noise in the house, and that I brought in
a lot of mud when I came back from
playing in the park, and that I left my
clothes lying about, and that I talked
and laughed too loudly. Aunt Hulda
kept saying it was an unlucky day when
I came to them. Uncle Olaf said nothing
. . . Yes! He did say, 'Go away! I can't
stand the sight of you.'

I spent most of my time at Ben's. His
daddy very often had chats with him
and helped him to build model
aeroplanes, and drew marks on the
kitchen door to show how much Ben

had grown, and things like that. Ben was allowed to laugh and talk and leave his clothes about as much as he liked. His daddy loved him just the same. And all the boys were welcome to play in Ben's home. Nobody was allowed to come home with me, because Aunt Hulda said she could not endure having children running in and out. Uncle Olaf agreed. 'We've got as much as we can stand with *this* brat around,' he said.

Sometimes when I had gone to bed I used to lie there wishing Ben's daddy was mine too. Then I would wonder who was my real daddy, and why I could not live with him and my mummy instead of being in the Children's Home, or having to stay with Aunt Hulda and Uncle Olaf. Aunt Hulda told me that my mummy had died when I was born. 'Who your father was, no-one knows,' she said, 'but it's easy enough to guess

that he was a good-for-nothing.' I hated
Aunt Hulda for speaking like that about
my father. Perhaps it was true that my
mother died when I was born, but I *knew*
that my father wasn't a good-for-
nothing. Sometimes, in bed, I lay crying
for him.

One person who was kind to me was
Mrs Lundy in the fruit shop. She used to
give me sweets and fruit.

Now, I can't help wondering who Mrs
Lundy really is. You see, it all began with
her on that day in October last year.

That day Aunt Hulda said to me
several times that it was an ill wind that
had brought me. A few minutes before 6
o'clock she told me to run down to a
baker's in Queen's Road to buy some
buns that she specially liked. I put on my
red cap and dashed off.

When I passed the fruit shop Mrs
Lundy was standing in the doorway. She

stroked my cheek and looked at me intently for a long time. Then she said, 'Would you like an apple?'

'Yes, *please*,' I said. So she gave me a lovely red apple that looked awfully good, and said, 'Will you mail a card for me?'

'Oh, yes,' I said.

She wrote a few lines on a card and handed it to me. 'Goodbye, Karl Anders Nilsson,' said Mrs Lundy. 'Goodbye.'

It sounded strange. She never used to call me anything but Andy.

I ran off to the mailbox a few houses away. Just as I was going to drop the card into the box I noticed that it shone and glowed like fire. Yes, the words that Mrs Lundy had written glowed like fire! I couldn't help reading them. This is what it said on the card:

To the King,
Farawayland.

The one whom you have long sought
is on his way. He travels by day and by
night and carries in his hand the sign —
the golden apple.

I didn't understand a word of it, but it
sent shivers up and down my spine. I
quickly dropped the card in the box.

Who was travelling by day and by
night? Who was carrying a golden apple
in his hand?

Then I caught sight of the apple that
Mrs Lundy had given me. And the apple
was made of gold! I had in my hand a
golden apple!

I nearly burst into tears — not quite,
but nearly. I felt so lonely. I went and sat
on a seat in the park. There wasn't
anyone there. Everybody had gone
home for supper. It was almost dark

among the trees and it rained a little.
But in the houses round the park there
were lights everywhere. I could see the
light from Ben's window, too. He was
sitting inside eating pease pudding and
pancakes with his daddy and mummy. It
seemed to me that behind every window
with a light shining from it there were
children at home together with their
daddies and mummies. Only *I* was
sitting out here in the dark. Alone!
Alone, holding a golden apple that I
didn't know what to do with.

I put the apple carefully on the seat
beside me and left it there while I
thought. There was a street light near
and the light fell on me and the apple.
But the light also fell on something that
was lying on the ground. It was an
ordinary beer bottle, empty, of course.
Someone had pushed a piece of wood
into the neck – one of the small children

who played in the park in the afternoons, I suppose. I picked up the bottle and looked at the label, which said, 'Stockholm Breweries Ltd., Pale Ale.' And just as I read it I noticed something moving inside the bottle.

I once borrowed a book called *A Thousand and One Nights* from the library, and it told about a genie who was shut in a bottle. But that was far away in Arabia, of course, and thousands of years ago, and I don't suppose that the genie was in an ordinary beer bottle. It's probably quite rare for genies to be in the beer bottles from Stockholm Breweries. But there was one in this bottle. It *was* a genie, truly, sitting inside the bottle. I could see he wanted to get out. He pointed to the wooden peg that blocked the neck of the bottle and looked at me imploringly. Of course, I wasn't really used to genies, so I was

almost too scared to pull out the
wooden peg. But I did, and with a great
roar the genie rushed out of the bottle
and began to grow very big – so big
that at last he was taller than all the
houses round the park. That's what
genies do: they can shrink so small that
there's enough room for them in bottles,
and the next moment they can become
as big as houses.

You can't imagine how frightened I
was. I shook with fright. The genie spoke
to me. His voice was a great roar, and I
thought at once Aunt Hulda and Uncle
Olaf ought to hear it; they are always
saying *I* speak too loudly.

'Child,' the genie said to me, 'you have
released me from my prison. You shall
name your reward.'

I didn't want a reward for pulling out
a small wooden peg. The genie told me
that he had come to Stockholm the

night before and had crept into the bottle to sleep. You see, genies can't imagine a better sleeping place than a bottle. But, while he was asleep, someone had blocked the way out. So, if I hadn't saved him, he might have had to stay in the bottle for a thousand years until the wooden peg had rotted.

'That would have displeased my lord the King,' said the genie, almost to himself, it seemed.

Then I plucked up courage and asked, 'Genie, where do you come from?'

He was silent for a moment. Then he said, 'I come from Farawayland.'

He said it so loudly that it rang and thundered in my head; and something in his voice made me long for that land. I felt as if I couldn't live if I didn't go there. I stretched my arms up toward the genie and cried, 'Take me with you! *Please* take me to Farawayland!

Someone is waiting for me there.'

The genie shook his head. Then I held
out the golden apple toward him and
the genie gave a loud cry. 'You carry in
your hand the sign! You are the one that
I have come to fetch. You are the one
that the King has so long been seeking.'

He bent down and lifted me in his
arms. Round us were the sound of bells
and the roar of thunder as we rose into
the air. We left the park far below us –
we left the gloomy park and all the
houses where there were lights in the
windows and where the children were
having supper with their daddies and
mummies, while I, Karl Anders Nilsson,
soared above, under the stars.

We flew high above the clouds and
we travelled faster than lightning and
with a roar louder than thunder. Stars
and moons and suns sparkled round us.
At times all was black as night, and at

other times so dazzingly bright and white that I had to shut my eyes.

'He travels by day and by night,' I whispered to myself. That was what it had said on the card.

Suddenly the genie stretched out his arm and pointed to something far away – something green that was lying in clear, blue water and in bright sunshine.

'Now you can see Farawayland,' said the genie.

We sank down towards the green island.

It was an island swimming in the sea, and in the air was the scent of a thousand roses and lilies and a strange music which was more beautiful than any other music in the world. A great white palace lay close to the shore, and we landed there.

A man came striding along the water's edge. It was *my father the King!*

I recognized him as soon as I saw him.
I knew he was my father. He opened his
arms and I ran straight into them. He
held me close for a long time. We didn't
say anything. I just kept my arms clasped
round his neck as tightly as I could.

Oh, how I wished Aunt Hulda could
have seen my father the King, how
handsome he was and how his clothes
glittered with gold and diamonds. His
face was like the face of Ben's daddy,
only more handsome. It was a pity Aunt
Hulda couldn't see him; then she would
have seen that my daddy was no good-
for-nothing.

Aunt Hulda was right when she said
that my mummy died when I was born;
and just imagine – the stupid people in
the Children's Home never thought of
telling my father the King where I was!
He has sought me for nine long years. I
am glad that I've come home at last.

★

I have been here for quite a long time
now. It's such fun all day. And every
evening my father the King comes to
my room and we build model
aeroplanes and talk.

I'm thriving and growing fast here in
Farawayland. My father the King draws
marks on the kitchen door every month
to show how much I've grown.

'Mio, my son! Goodness, how you've
grown again,' he says when we measure
me. 'Mio, my son,' he says, and it sounds
so kind and warm. So my name isn't
Andy at all, really.

'I was seeking you for nine long
years,' says my father the King. 'I often
lay awake at night saying to myself,
"Mio, my son." So I should know your
name well, shouldn't I?'

There you are. Calling me Andy was
a mistake, like everything else that

happened when I lived in North Street.
Now it has been put right.

I love my father the King, and he
loves me.

I wish Ben knew about all this. I think
I'll write and tell him about it and I'll
put the letter in a bottle. Then I'll put a
cork in the bottle and throw it in the
blue sea which is round Farawayland.
When Ben is with his daddy and
mummy at their seaside cottage in
Vaxholm perhaps the bottle will come
sailing along just when he's swimming.
That would be good. You see, I should
like Ben to know about all these strange
things that have happened to me. He
could ring up the police, too, and tell
them that Karl Anders Nilsson, whose
real name is Mio, is in safe keeping in
Farawayland with his father the King,
and all is well with him.

This story is by Astrid Lindgren.

The Witch at the Window

If Lucinda had not been born with a silver spoon in her mouth, it must at least have been a silver-plated one. And probably with a pattern of pink enamelled roses as well. For Lucinda was a very 'pink roses' little girl. She had pink roses on her party dress and pink roses on her bedroom wallpaper. The paintwork of her bedroom, too, was sugary pink.

'Sugar and spice and all things nice,' cooed her grandmother fondly. 'That's what little girls are made of.'

Lucinda did not have to share her grandmother with any brother or sister, or any cousins either. Because she was the only child in the family, all her aunts and uncles made a great fuss of her and gave her lovely presents at birthday and Christmas times — white fluffy toys and pretty rings and necklaces. All, that is, except Aunt Morag. Aunt Morag loomed like the unwanted fairy godmother at all family gatherings. While the rest of the adults sipped sweet sherry and talked about the state of the weather and the Stock Exchange, Aunt Morag sat silent and glowering in a haze of cigarette smoke. Lucinda's mother would tut and open the doors and windows, but she never dared to ask Aunt Morag to smoke outside.

Once, Lucinda and her parents had actually been to stay with Aunt Morag at her ivy-strangled cottage in the country. It had been a terrible experience. Lucinda had had to wash in cold water and suffer at night in a narrow, lumpy bed, staring in terror at a cobweb on the ceiling, expecting that at any moment a hairy black spider would descend from it and land on her face. Aunt Morag had made her get up at seven to feed squawking, vicious hens and a big fat pig which gave out disgusting grunting noises and kept pressing its filthy body against Lucinda. Aunt Morag told her a story about a neighbouring farmer who had fallen asleep in his pig-pen and how his favourite sow had started to eat his foot! It was with indescribable relief that Lucinda returned home to her own comfortable sunny room, and her big soft quilt with flowers and pierrots on it.

As her eighth birthday approached, Lucinda did wonder once or twice what her present from Aunt Morag would be. Last year's present, a chemistry set, still lay untouched in its box. Lucinda had been born at the loveliest time of the year, of course — the month of May — and as her birthday fell this time on a Saturday, her mother prepared her a special birthday breakfast and arranged all the colourful and beribboned packages from doting aunts and uncles carefully round it.

It was obvious, thought Lucinda, which present was from Aunt Morag. Amidst the candy stripes and little shining stars and frilled rosettes sat a book-shaped object, hastily wrapped in brown paper and tied, Lucinda noted disdainfully, with the rough green string Aunt Morag used for her broad beans and dahlias. Lucinda decided to open the ugly brown parcel last — the other gifts looked so much more attractive. But

even as she oohed and aahed at the
silver bracelet, the china kitten, the box
of strawberry creams, Lucinda was
wondering, at the back of her mind, just
what sort of a book her least favourite
aunt had given her.

When she finally tore open the brown
paper and stared at the book, it was
with a sense of deep disappointment. She
had, at least, expected something
unusual. But all Aunt Morag had sent
was a copy of *Hansel and Gretel*. Hansel
and Gretel indeed! What a babyish
story! Surely Aunt Morag realized she
was eight years old now?

Lucinda had first heard *Hansel and
Gretel* when she was five and had not
liked it at all. She had not been able to
understand how the mother and father
in the story could deliberately lose their
children in the forest, no matter how
poor they might be. The deep forest had

frightened her and when she came to the part of the story where Hansel and Gretel find the gingerbread house, and the ugly old woman who turns out to be a witch – a witch who plans to roast the children in her oven and eat them! – she could listen no more. Lucinda's mother, alarmed at her sobs, hastily removed *Hansel and Gretel* and replaced it with a book called *Flower Fairies of the Dell*. And Lucinda had thought no more about Hansel and Gretel until her eighth birthday when, staring down at her present, she decided that Aunt Morag must surely have sent it out of spite.

To add insult to injury, there were not even words in the book. It was just a series of pictures – of the pop-up variety, which seemed to spring to life whenever one turned a page. The first page showed the woodcutter's cottage at the edge of the forest. The trees were very

realistic-looking. As the page opened
they trembled, as if a breeze was passing
through them. The second page showed
Hansel and Gretel in the deep, dark
forest. Lucinda shivered a little when she
saw that. But on the third page the
children were back home again. The
fourth page pictured an even deeper part
of the forest and the gingerbread house,
with its roof of marzipan and icing and
windows of frosted sugar. On the fifth
page one of the windows sprang open to
reveal a hideous witch. Lucinda
screamed and closed the book quickly.
She expected her mother to come
running into the room to ask what the
matter was, but her mother was having
words outside with the milkman, and
didn't hear her. Lucinda opened the
book at the fifth page a second time,
very slowly, peeped at the horrible grey-
faced crone with hair like matted rope,

and shut the book again.

That night, long after her light had been put out and her parents were downstairs talking, Lucinda opened the book and shone her torch into the witch's face.

'You don't frighten me,' she whispered, 'you don't frighten me at all!'

In the torchlight the witch's eyes shone green as glass. There was even a spot of saliva on her chin. Lucinda closed the book quickly, hurrying barefoot from the room. Her toes sank into the thick pile of the landing carpet. On the landing was a cupboard which her mother used for storing towels and linen. Lucinda pushed the book into the cupboard and closed the door firmly. Then she tiptoed back to bed, still trembling a little.

Later that night she dreamed that she was wandering about inside the book.

She was lost in the forest and hungry.
The trees overhead were gaunt and
dark, rustling like paper. The knots of the
trunks had faces on them. The floor of
the forest was slippery, like the surface of
a page.

'Face number five,' a voice kept
whispering. 'Face number five.'

Lucinda moved, with difficulty, to the
fifth tree and pressed the knot on its
bark. The wooden face seemed familiar.
Then, somehow, she had passed through
the tree and there in front of her was the
gingerbread house, glowing golden in
the darkness of the forest. She saw that
the pillars of the house were made of
twisted barley-sugar and her mouth
watered. She stretched out her hand to
break off a piece, but suddenly there was
Aunt Morag, actually smiling at her
from the window of the gingerbread
house. Aunt Morag beckoned, but as

Lucinda moved towards her the smile became a hideous scowl and her teeth rotted black as liquorice.

'It's the witch!' screamed Lucinda.

Aunt Morag set up a repulsive cackling. She reached out a claw-like hand and shook Lucinda, who awoke to find herself in bed and being shaken by her mother, with her own sweet smile and teeth as white as mint imperials.

'You've been dreaming,' whispered Lucinda's mother. 'Wake up now, gently does it. Why are you staring at me like that, darling? Is something wrong?'

Lucinda shook her head, but even as she cuddled up to her mother, she was half afraid of her turning into a witch as well. When morning came she fetched the book from the linen cupboard and, with half-closed eyes, cut out the witch from the window, scrunching her up into a tight little ball and dropping her into the waste paper basket.

After that, Lucinda lost interest in the present from Aunt Morag. It lay, unopened, at the back of her toy-shelf, throughout the months of June and July. In August came the school holidays and Lucinda, when deciding what to pack for the seaside, glanced at it again. But she felt no desire to open the book. The witch had gone, so there seemed no point in it.

They took Grandma with them to the hotel at the seaside, but Lucinda had a room to herself. The room was painted blue, with pretty sea-shell-patterned walls. There was a poodle made of seashells on the bedside table, and a tiny balcony with a view of the sea.

The weather was sunny, with a pleasant salty breeze. Lucinda paddled in the sea, and when the water lapped against her knees she felt very daring. Her mother and father read books under beach umbrellas and Grandma snoozed. One day a group of rather scruffy-looking boys started aiming pebbles into a nearby rockpool and the water splashed over Grandma's lap. Lucinda's father stood up angrily and the boys ran off, shouting with laughter.

'Rats and snails and puppy-dogs' tails,' muttered Grandma, mopping herself with a starched handkerchief. 'That's what little *boys* are made of.'

Towards the end of the first week of the holiday, Grandma decided to have her afternoon nap at the hotel while Lucinda and her mother and father went for a special trip in a steam train. They chugged through the gently undulating countryside. Cows and trees and farmers on red tractors sailed sedately past the windows. There were old-fashioned, brown-coloured prints above the seats of the train.

'Tickets, please,' said a man in a spankingly smart uniform. He smiled at Lucinda. 'Next stop Sandhaven.'

'I'm not sure that I *would* want steam trains back again,' said Lucinda's mother, as she negotiated the steep drop onto the platform. 'It does seem to create rather a lot of mess. Look at those smudges on your white dress, darling.'

The little station had boxes of brightly-coloured geraniums and a brown and gold metal sign which read WELCOME TO SANDHAVEN.

'It's like stepping back in time,' said Lucinda's father. 'It's a shame Grandma didn't come.'

The village seemed to be in league with the railway company. The little tea-shops offering scones and jam, the antique shops with their gleaming brasses, all had an olde-worlde look to them.

'I wonder if property is very expensive?' whispered Lucinda's mother. 'It would be rather nice to live here, wouldn't it, John?'

Then, as they turned a corner into a side-street, she cried out, 'Oh, look at that sweetshop. Isn't it lovely?'

Lucinda stared. The shop was painted up like a golden gingerbread house. The pillars on either side of the door were twisted like barley sugar, and the roof shone like an iced cake. Behind frosted windows, with round humbugs set into them, stood rows of jars of multicoloured sweets.

'We must buy something,' laughed Lucinda's mother. 'It takes me back to my childhood. It's a Hansel and Gretel house.'

Lucinda followed her mother and father into the shop slowly, nervously. It was true there had been no hideous face at the window, but what might be lurking in the dark corners of the quaint little shop, behind the sherbet dips, the jars of jelly beans?

'I'll be with you in a moment,' called out a pleasant, sing-song voice, and out of the shadows came a plump, rosy-faced, smiling little old woman with candid blue eyes and hair scraped back into a neat bun.

Lucinda breathed a huge sigh of relief and, as her parents were enjoying themselves so much, she began to enjoy herself, too. She chose half a pound of striped humbugs, three dear little white sugar mice with pink noses and, yes, as her fears settled themselves for ever, two long, elaborate coils of blackest liquorice. The little old lady chatted amiably about this and that as she weighed out the sweets for them, and when they left she waved goodbye from between the sugar portals, her smile as warm as fudge straight from the oven.

Lucinda's mother had bought a bag of big, squashy marshmallows, and on the train going back she offered them round.

'So soon after that enormous cream tea,' she sighed. 'I am making a pig of myself. Would you like one, Lucinda dear?'

Lucinda shook her head. She felt too full for marshmallows. I might, she thought, manage a minty humbug, though.

Feeling stickily into the paper bag, trying to dislodge one humbug from another, she thought she felt something move. The humbugs seemed to have a different feel to them — colder, more fragile, somehow. And the stickiness underneath them — wasn't that more of a slime? Peering into the bag, she saw with amazement that it was full of snails — moving snails with tiny horns and black and yellow striped shells on their backs.

Suddenly the three sugar mice leapt from her pocket. They skittled across the floor of the compartment, baring their teeth like angry rats, growing larger, becoming furry.

The coils of liquorice slithered, snake-like, to join them — lurching, wriggling, *wagging* almost, just like—

A whistle blew, high and shrill, the screeching of a banshee. Lucinda froze. She could hear it now — the witch's laughter. She could see the grey, gnarled grinning face at the window of the train. The laughter went on and on, high-pitched and hysterical. The whistle blew like a chorus of banshees, the face turned into the face of Aunt Morag, and the train plunged headlong into a long, dark, never-ending tunnel.

This story is by Wendy Eyton.

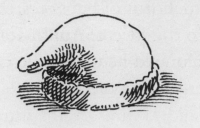

The Little Blue Caps

Now this is the tale of a fisherman who sailed through the air instead of the water. And this is the way I tell it.

Once upon a time there was a fisherman. His name was Ian. Every day he used to go out fishing in his boat. But one day the sea was so rough and so wild that he couldn't go fishing. So he decided he would mend his boat instead.

He began looking about on the hill for a good, strong piece of wood, just the size he needed to mend his boat. He was looking and looking and not finding it at all, when a mist came up and the day began to grow dark. 'Oh, I'd better give up looking for the wood, and get back home,' he said to himself. 'If I stay on the hillside till the mist gets thick, I shan't be able to see where I am, and I'll get lost and never see my little house again.'

So he stopped looking for the wood to mend his boat, and started off home. But the mist was already thick, and he did get lost.

Suddenly through the clouds of mist he came right up to a house. He knew there was someone in because there was a light in the window. He banged on the door. Thump! 'Please let me in,' he called. 'I'm lost in the mist.' But no-one came. He banged again. Thump! 'Please let me in. I'm lost in the mist.' But still no-one came. So he banged louder than ever, banged and banged till his hand hurt. Thump! Thump! Thump! 'Please, please let me in. I'm lost in the mist.'

And then, at last, the door opened a teeny crack. And there was a little old woman, peeping at him with her eyes screwed up. 'What do you want?' she said crossly.

'I want to come in,' said Ian. 'It's thick with mist, and dark out here, and I'm lost, so please will you let me come in to stay till morning, when I can see my way home again?'

The old woman peeped at him and sniffed and grumbled. But at last she said, 'All right. You can come in.'

So in he came, right into the kitchen. There was a big, warm fire burning, and that was good, and at each side of the fire sat another little woman – three little old women in the house together. And they never said a word to Ian, not any of them, not one word. So he didn't say a word either. He lay down on the floor by the side of the fire and pretended to go to sleep. But he didn't really go to sleep. He watched the little old women.

Now the little old women thought he really was asleep. So they went to a big box in the corner of the room and they lifted the lid. Then one of them took out a blue woolly cap, and she put it on her head, and she said, 'Carlisle!' And do you know, she vanished away! She'd gone! She wasn't there any more.

Then the second little woman took a blue woolly cap out of the box and put it on, and she said, 'Carlisle!' And *she* vanished. She wasn't there any more.

And then the third little woman took a blue woolly cap out of the chest, and popped it on her head and said, 'Carlisle!' and *she* vanished. *She* wasn't there any more.

'What an extraordinary thing,' said Ian. 'First there were three little old women here, and now there are none at all. Only me. I wonder if there are any more blue woolly caps in that chest?' So he had a look. There was. Just one more.

He took it out, and he popped it on his head and said, 'Carlisle!' – just like the little old women. And *he* vanished. He went flying and swirling and crossing and curling away and away and away, to goodness knows where. Then suddenly down he crashed, with a bump and a thump and a clackety clump. Where was he? Down in a cellar with the three old women.

And all around them were bottles of different kinds and different shapes and different sizes. And the three little old women were tasting all the bottles and having a party.

But when they saw Ian come down

with a bump and a thump and a clackety clump in the middle of them, they settled their blue woolly caps on their heads and fast as fast shouted 'Kintail, back again!' And they were gone, first one, then two, then three.

'What an extraordinary thing,' said Ian. 'First there were three old women. And now there are none. Only me.'

Well, this time Ian didn't want to follow them. He was quite happy where he was. He tasted all the bottles, and he sipped them and licked them and drank them, till at last he had drunk so much and got so sticky that he fell fast asleep.

Now would you believe it, the place where Ian was lying fast asleep among all this shocking muddle was the Bishop of Carlisle's wine cellar. You remember the three old women had shouted, 'Carlisle!' when they had popped on their little blue caps. Well, there you are!

Naturally, when the Bishop of Carlisle's servants came down the next morning and saw all the mess – all the broken bottles, and the corks out, and the stickiness, and the pools and the puddles and the muddle – they were very angry indeed. 'You bad, *bad* man!' they shouted at Ian, and they took him off to the Bishop.

'Take off your little blue cap,' they shouted at him. 'It's very rude to keep on your cap when you talk to the Bishop.' And they snatched it off. Then they tied him to a big piece of wood.

Ian was very frightened. He didn't know what the Bishop would do to him for breaking into his wine cellar in the middle of the night and making such a mess there.

So what did he do? He said, 'Please, sir, may I have my cap back?' And the second the Bishop gave it him back, he

popped it on his head and shouted,
'Kintail, back again,' just like the three
old women had done. And he vanished.
Which was a very good thing, for
goodness knows what the Bishop would
have done to him.

He went flying and swirling and
crossing and curling away and away
and away, to goodness knows where.
Then down he came with a bump and a
thump and a clackety clump. There he
was back on his own hill in the bright
morning. Only I'm afraid he was tied to
a big piece of wood.

Well, luckily he saw an old man
coming up the hill, so he called out,
'Please, old man, will you untie me from
this piece of wood?' And the old man
said, 'Of course,' and untied him right
away – at least, as soon as he could get
up to him, because old people go rather
slowly up hills, and his old fingers were

rather stiff for untying knots.

Ian said, 'Thank you,' of course. And then the old man said, 'Whatever did you want with that piece of wood?' And Ian remembered what he wanted with it. He remembered that right at the very beginning of this story, he'd been looking for a piece of wood to mend his boat. And now he had it. It was just the right size.

'That's for mending my boat,' he told the old man. 'The Bishop of Carlisle gave it to me.'

'Fancy that!' said the old man. Then they both said, 'Goodbye,' and they each went home.

This story is by Leila Berg.

The Willow Baby

You know this as well as I do but it can't be said often enough. You must be careful of the Little People. If they take a fancy to you, of course, that's well and good. But if they are feeling full of mischief, that's a different story. Like the story about the willow baby.

There was once a young mother who was always talking about her new baby son. Of course all new mothers think their child is the prettiest in the world but it is not always wise to say so. Not out loud anyway.

'Just look at him,' she would coo. 'Isn't he a treasure? Isn't he the most gorgeous little pet you ever saw?'

'Hush!' said her friends. 'Be careful.' They looked round nervously. 'Don't say such things.'

'But it's true!' protested the mother. 'There's not another baby so beautiful.'

'Don't say another word,' warned the other women. 'You never know who may be listening.'

The young mother just laughed. She knew her baby was beautiful and, better still, he was healthy and contented.

One morning, when it was fine and pleasant, she decided to go onto the hill to gather berries. She wrapped the baby in a shawl, took a basket and began the climb. Before long, she discovered a circle of fresh, green grass, surrounded by sheltering bushes full of fruit. She spread out the shawl and put her baby on the soft grass.

He was perfectly happy. He gurgled and held up his tiny fingers, looking at them in amazement. He was perfectly content.

The mother began to pick the berries. She was happy, too. Every now and then, she would glance back but the baby was chuckling and kicking and watching the birds in the bushes, so she continued to fill her basket.

Now, you know how it is with picking berries. There is always a better patch a little further on and although she continued to call out to the baby, she was moving slowly away from him.

She stopped suddenly when she heard the strangest cry. It wasn't a bird but it didn't sound like her baby. Then the baby began to scream.

She quickly ran back to him and as soon as he saw her, he began to howl. He howled louder than he had ever done before. His face had become red and wrinkled and he kicked angrily.

The young mother was very frightened. She wrapped him in the shawl and hurried home. But he would not settle in his cradle and soon the poor young woman was quite desperate. Hour after hour, he kicked and screamed and the only moments of peace she had was when she was feeding him.

It seemed that he had suddenly become very hungry, even greedy. He drank all his milk and yelled for more. She made him porridge: one bowl, two bowls, three. Surely such a young baby should not be eating so much? She walked up and down all night with him over her shoulder and still he would not settle. She had to make him another big pot of porridge.

In the morning, an old woman came to her door. She made baskets from the

willow withies she carried on her cart.
The young woman had bought baskets
from her before and knew she was a
Wise Woman, from beyond the
mountains.

'My dear,' said the woman, kindly,
'you look very tired. Are you ill?'

At this, the poor young mother burst
into tears and told her how her lovely
baby had changed and how she could
do nothing to make him happy.

The older woman listened to the baby
crying. It was a horrid, hoarse sound
and she went over to look at him.

'I see,' she said. 'I supposed you often
boasted about your baby?'

'I used to,' sobbed the mother.

'Quite so,' she nodded. 'It's never a
good idea. There are ears everywhere.'

'He hardly seems the same child,' said
the mother, wiping her eyes on her
apron.

'That's because he isn't,' the old lady replied. 'This is a changeling. Did you leave your baby alone?'

'Never!' she cried. 'Well, perhaps. When I was picking berries on the hill, I wandered further than I meant to.'

'That would be it.' The Wise Woman seemed sure now. 'No doubt you put him down in a fairy circle and the Little People stole him away. They've put some little goblin in his place, by the looks of it.'

At that, the mother began to cry and shriek so loudly that the old woman put her hands over her ears. 'For goodness sake! What's the use of all that? Hold your noise and let me think. Run outside to my cart and bring me some willow. I have some weaving to do.'

The Wise Woman sat by the fire and began to make a basket but it was a strange one. By the time her quick fingers had stopped twisting and pushing, the basket had two arms, two legs and a head. In fact, it looked like a willow baby.

The changeling began to scream again.

'Feed him,' ordered the old lady. 'As much as you can. I'll heat the cauldron.'

While the mother fed the baby, the woman fed the fire and soon the cauldron was bubbling.

'Now pass me the shawl,' she whispered, 'the same one as you used on the mountain when you were picking berries.'

She wrapped the willow baby in the shawl and then spoke louder.

'Has he finished his porridge?' she asked. 'Well, well, give him another bowl. Give him some eggs and plenty of bread.'

The baby gobbled everything

and then howled again.

'What a splendid appetite!' She was still talking loudly. 'Have you any mashed potato in the house? And what about that chop that you were going to give your husband for dinner?'

'Should I really give him something like that?' asked the young mother.

'Oh course,' said the Wise Woman, 'because when he's fat enough, we'll put him in this pot and have him for dinner. In fact, he's ready NOW!'

As she said it, she plunged the willow baby, shawl and all, into the cauldron.

The changeling sat bolt upright, looking much older than it ought and screeched, 'Come and fetch me, Mother! They're going to eat me for dinner!'

There was a frenzied scuffling in the chimney. Soot scattered everywhere. Down the chimney flew a fairy woman and she was carrying the young mother's real child.

'Here, take what's yours,' she cried, 'and I'll take my own!'

And snatching up the changeling, she flew straight out of the window.

'That's done, then,' said the Wise Woman, shaking the soot from her skirt. 'Now take care in future. Never praise your child when the Little People might hear you.'

So now you know how it is. The young mother had five more children, equally bonny, but she never told them how beautiful they were – except when she whispered in their ears as she kissed them goodnight.

This story is by Pat Thomson.

The Dead Moon

Long ago, the moon used to shine just as she shone last night. And when she shone, she cast her light over the marshland: the great pools of black water, and the creeping trickles of green water, and the squishy mounds that sucked anyone in who stepped on them. She lit up the whole swamp so that people could walk about almost as safely as in broad daylight.

But when the moon did not shine, out came the Things that live in the darkness. They wormed around, waiting for a chance to harm those people who were not safe at home beside their own hearths. Harm and mishap and evil: bogles and dead things and crawling horrors: they all appeared on the nights when the moon did not shine.

The moon came to hear of this. And being kind and good, as she surely is, shining for us night after night instead of going to sleep, she was upset at what was going on behind her back. She said to herself, 'I'll see what's going on for myself. Maybe it's not as bad as people make out.'

And sure enough, at the end of the month the moon stepped down onto the earth, wearing a black cloak and a black hood over her yellow shining hair. She went straight to the edge of the bogland and looked about her.

There was water here, and water there; waving tussocks, trembling mounds, and great black snags of peat all twisted and bent; and in front of her, everything was dark – dark except for the pools glimmering under the stars and the light that came from the moon's own white feet, poking out beneath her black cloak.

The moon walked forward, right into the middle of the marsh, always looking to left and to right, and over her shoulders. Then she saw she had company, and strange company at that.

'Witches,' whispered the moon, and the witches grinned at her as they rode past on their huge black cats.

'The eye,' she whispered, and the evil eye glowered at her from the deepest darkness.

'Will-o'-the wykes,' whispered the moon, and the will-o'-the-wykes danced around her with their lanterns swinging on their backs.

'The dead,' she whispered, and dead folk rose out of the water. Their faces were white and twisted and hell-fire blazed in their empty eye sockets, and they stared blindly around them.

'And dead hands,' whispered the moon. Slimy dripping dead hands slithered about, beckoning and pointing, so cold and wet that they made the moon's skin crawl.

The moon drew her cloak more tightly around her and trembled. But she was resolved not to go back without seeing all there was to be seen. So on she went, stepping as lightly as the summer wind from tuft to tuft between the greedy gurgling water holes.

Just as the moon came up to a big black pool, her foot slipped. With both hands she grabbed at a snag of peat to steady herself, and save herself from tumbling in. But as soon as she touched

it, the snag twined itself round her wrists like a pair of handcuffs, and gripped her so that she couldn't escape. The moon pulled and twisted and fought, but it was no good; she was trapped, completely trapped. Then she looked about her, and wondered if anyone at all would be out that night, and pass by, and help her. But she saw nothing except shifting, flurrying evil Things, coming and going, toing and froing, all of them busy and all of them up to no good.

After a while, as the moon stood trembling in the dark, she heard something calling in the distance – a voice that called and called, and then died away in a sob. Then the voice was raised again in a screech of pain and fear, and called and called, until the marshes were haunted by that pitiful crying sound. Then the moon heard the sound of steps, someone floundering along, squishing through the mud, slipping on the tufts. And, through the darkness, she saw a pair of hands catching at the snags and tussocks, and a white face with wide, terrified eyes.

It was a man who had strayed into the marsh. The grinning bogles and dead folk and creeping horrors crawled and crowded around him; voices mocked him; the dead hands plucked at him. And, ahead of him, the will-o'-the-wykes dangled their lanterns, and shook with glee as they lured him further and further away from the safe path over the swamp. Trembling with fear and loathing at the Things all around him, the man struggled on towards the flickering lights ahead of him that looked as if they would give him help and bring him home in safety.

'You over there!' yelled the man. 'You! I'm caught in the swamp. Can you hear me?' His voice rose to a shriek. 'Help! You over there! Help! God and Mary save me from these horrors.' Then the man paused, and sobbed and moaned, and called on the saints and wise women and on God Himself to save him from the swamp.

But then the man shrieked again as the slimy slithery Things crawled around him and reared up so that he could not even see the false lights, the will-o'-the-wykes, ahead of him.

As if matters were not bad enough already, the horrors began to take on all sorts of shapes; beautiful girls winked at him with their bright eyes, and stretched out soft helping hands towards him. But when he tried to catch hold of them, they changed in his grip to slimy things and shapeless worms, and evil voices derided him and mocked him with foul laughter. Then all the bad thoughts that the man had ever had, and all the bad things that he had ever done, came and whispered in his ears, and danced about, and shouted out all the secrets that were buried in his own heart. The man shrieked and sobbed with pain and shame, and the horrors crawled and gibbered around him and mocked him.

When the poor moon saw that the man was getting nearer and nearer to the deep water holes and deadly sinking mud, and further and further from firm ground, she was so angry and so sorry for him that she struggled and fought and pulled harder than ever. She still couldn't break loose. But with all her twisting and tugging, her black hood fell back from her shining yellow hair. And the beautiful light that came from it drove away the darkness.

The man cried for joy to see God's own light again. And at once the evil

Things, unable to stand the light, scurried and delved and dropped away into their dark corners. They left the man and fled. And the man could see where he was, and where the path was, and which way to take to get out of the marsh.

He was in such a hurry to get away from the sinking mud and the swamp, and all the Things that lived there, that he scarcely glanced at the brave light that shone from the beautiful shining yellow hair streaming out over the black cloak, and falling into the water at his very feet.

And the moon herself was so taken up with saving the man, and so happy that he was back on the right path, that she completely forgot she needed help herself. For she was still trapped in the clutches of the black snag.

The man made off, gasping and

stumbling and exhausted, sobbing for joy, running for his life out of the terrible swamp. Then the moon realized how much she would have liked to go with him. She shook with terror. And she pulled and fought as if she were mad, until, worn out with tugging, she fell to her knees at the foot of the snag. As the moon lay there, panting, the black hood fell forward over her head. And although she tried to toss it back again, it caught in her hair and would not move.

Out went that beautiful light, and back came the darkness with all its evil creatures, screeching and howling. They crowded around the moon, mocking at her and snatching at her and striking her; shrieking with rage and spite; swearing with foul mouths, spitting and snarling. They knew she was their old enemy, the brave bright moon, who drove them back into their corners and

stopped them from doing all their
wicked deeds. They swarmed all around
her and made a ghastly clapperdatch.
The poor moon crouched in the mud,
trembling and sick at heart, and
wondered when they would make an
end of their caterwauling, and an end of
her.

'Curse you!' yelled the witches.
'You've spoiled our spells all this last
year.'

'And you keep us in our narrow
coffins at night,' moaned the dead folk.

'And you send us off to skulk in the
corners,' howled the bogles.

Then all the Things shouted in one
voice, 'Ho, ho! Ho, ho!'

The tussocks shook and the water
gurgled and the Things raised their
voices again.

'We'll poison her — poison her!'
shrieked the witches.

'Ho, ho!' howled the Things again.

'We'll smother her – smother her!' whispered the crawling horrors, and they twined themselves around her knees.

'Ho, ho!' shouted all the rest of them.

'We'll strangle her – strangle her!' screeched the dead hands, and they plucked at her throat with cold fingers.

'Ho, ho!' they all yelled again.

And the dead folk writhed and grinned all around her, and chuckled to themselves. 'We'll bury you – bury you down with us in the black earth!'

Once more they all shouted, full of spite and ill will. The poor moon crouched low, and wished she were dead and done for.

The Things of the darkness fought and squabbled over what should be done with the moon until the sky in the east paled and turned grey; it drew near to dawn. When they saw that, they were all

worried that they would not have time
to do their worst. They caught hold of
the moon with horrid bony fingers, and
laid her deep in the water at the foot of
the snag.

The dead folk held her down while
the bogles found a strange big stone.
They rolled it right on top of her to stop
her from getting up again.

Then the Things told two will-o'-the-
wykes to take turns at standing on the
black snag to watch over the moon and
make sure she lay safe and still. They
didn't want her to get away and spoil
their sport with her light, or help the
poor marshmen at night to avoid the
sinking mud and the water holes.

Then, as the grey light began to
brighten, the shapeless Things fled into
their dark corners; the dead folk crept
back into the water, or crammed
themselves into their coffins; and the

witches went home to work their spells and curses. And the green slimy water shone in the light of dawn as if nothing, no wicked or evil creature, had ever gone near it.

There lay the poor moon, dead and buried in the marsh, until someone would set her free. And who knew even where to look for her?

Days passed, nights passed, and it was time for the birth of the new moon. People put pennies in their pockets, and straw in their caps, so as to be ready for it. They looked up at the sky uneasily, for the moon was a good friend to the marsh folk, and they were only too happy when she began to wax, and the pathways were safe again, and the evil Things were driven back by her blessed light into the darkness and the water holes.

But day followed day and the new moon never rose. The nights were always dark and the evil Things were worse than ever. It was not safe at all to travel alone, and the boggarts crept and wailed round the houses of the marsh folk. They peeped through the windows and tipped the latches until the poor people had to burn candles and lamps all night to stop the horrors from crossing their thresholds and forcing their way in.

The bogles and other creatures seemed to have lost all their fear. They howled and laughed and screeched around the hamlet, as if they were trying to wake the dead themselves. The marsh folk listened, and sat trembling and shaking by their fires. They couldn't sleep or rest or put a foot out of doors, and one dark and dreary night followed another.

When days turned into weeks and the

new moon still did not rise, the villagers were upset and afraid. A group of them went to the wise woman who lived in the old mill, and asked her if she could find out where the moon had gone.

The wise woman looked in the cauldron, and in the mirror, and in the Book. 'Well,' she said, 'it's queer. I can't tell you for sure what has happened to her.'

She shook her head and the marsh folk shook their heads.

'It's only dark, dead,' said the wise woman. 'You must wait a while, and let me think about it, and then maybe I'll be able to help you. If you hear of anything, any clue, come by and tell me. And,' said the wise woman, 'be sure to put a pinch of salt, a straw and a button on the doorstep each night. The horrors will never cross it then, light or no light.'

Then the marsh folk left the wise

woman and the mill and went their
separate ways. As the days went by, and
the new moon never rose, they talked
and talked. They wondered
and pondered and worried and guessed,
at home and in the inn and in the fields
around the marshland.

One day, sitting on the great settle in
the inn, a group of men were discussing
the whereabouts of the moon, and
another customer, a man from the far
end of the marshland, smoked and
listened to the talk. Suddenly this
stranger sat up and slapped his knee.
'My Lord!' he said. 'I'd clean forgotten,
but I reckon I know where the moon
is.'

All the men sitting on the settle turned
round to look at him. Then the stranger
told them about how he had got lost in
the marsh and how, when he was almost
dead with fright, the light had shone

out, and all the evil Things fled from it, and he had found the marsh-path and got home safely.

'And I was so terrified,' said the stranger, 'that I didn't really look to see where the light had come from. But I do remember it was white and soft like the moon herself.

'And this light came from something dark,' said the man, 'standing near a black snag in the water.' He paused and puffed at his pipe. 'I didn't really look,' he said again, 'but I think I remember a shining face and yellow hair in the middle of the dazzle. It had a sort of kind look, like the old moon herself above the marshland at night.'

At once all the men got up from the settle and went back to the wise woman. They told her everything the stranger had said. She listened and then stared once more, stared long into the cauldron and into the Book. Then she nodded. 'It's still dark,' she said, 'and I can't see anything for sure. But do as I tell you, and you can find out for yourselves. All of you must meet just before night falls. Put a stone in your mouths,' said the wise woman, 'and take a hazel twig in your hands, and say never a word until you're safe home again. Then step out and fear nothing! Make your way into the middle of the marsh, until you find a coffin, a candle and a cross.' The wise woman stared at the circle of anxious faces around her. 'Then you won't be far from your moon,' she said. 'Search, and maybe you'll find her.'

The men looked at each other and scratched their heads.

'But where will we find her, mother?' asked one.

'And which of us must go?' asked another.

'And the bogles, won't they do for us?' said a third.

'Houts!' exclaimed the wise woman impatiently. 'You parcel of fools! I can tell you no more. Do as I've told you and fear nothing.' She glared at the men. 'And if you don't like my advice, stay at home. Do without your moon if that's what you want.'

The next day, at dusk, all the men in the hamlet came out of their houses. Each had a stone in his mouth and a hazel twig in his hand, and each was feeling nervous and creepy.

Then the men stumbled and stuttered along the paths out into the middle of the marsh. It was so dark that they could see almost nothing. But they heard sighings and flusterings, and they could feel wet fingers touching them. On they went, peering about for the coffin, the candle and the cross, until they came near to the pool next to the great snag where the moon lay buried.

All at once they stopped in their tracks, quaking and shaking and scared. For there they saw the great stone, half in and half out of the water, looking for all the world like a strange big coffin. And at its head stood the black snag, stretching out its two arms in a dark gruesome cross. A little light flickered on it, like a dying candle.

The men knelt down in the mud, and crossed themselves, and said the Lord's Prayer to themselves. First they said it forwards because of the cross, and then they said it backwards, to keep the bogles away. But they mouthed it all without so much as a whisper, for they knew the evil Things would catch them if they did not do as the wise woman had told them.

Then the men shuffled to the edge of

the water. They took hold of the big stone, and levered it up, and for one moment, just one moment, they saw a strange and beautiful face looking up at them, and looking so grateful, out of the black water.

But then the light came so quickly, and was so white and shining, that the men stepped back, stunned by it, and by the great angry wail raised by the fleeing horrors. And the very next minute, when they came to their senses, the men saw the full moon in the sky. She was as bright and beautiful and kind as ever, shining and smiling down at them; she showed the marsh and the marsh-paths as clearly as daylight and stole into every nook and cranny, as though she would have liked to drive the darkness and the bogles away for ever.

Then the marsh folk went home with light hearts and happy. And, ever since, the moon has shone more brightly and clearly over the marshland than anywhere else.

This story is by Kevin Crossley-Holland.

A CHEST OF STORIES FOR NINE YEAR OLDS
Collected by Pat Thomson

Open up this chest of stories and you will find . . . a starving boy rescued by a cat, a prince who marries a tortoise, a little boy who likes being frightened, kidnappers from space, a bony-legged witch, and many other weird and wonderful characters. You won't want to stop reading until you get right to the bottom of the chest!

'A good mix of stories and styles well suited to the stated age group . . . there is something here for everybody'
The Times Educational Supplement

0 552 52758 0

CORGI BOOKS

A SACKFUL OF STORIES FOR EIGHT YEAR OLDS
Collected by Pat Thomson

Delve into this sack of stories and you will find . . . a Martian wearing Granny's jumper, that well-known comic fairy-tale pair Handsel and Gristle, a unicorn, a leprechaun, a princess who is a pig, and many other strange and exciting characters. You won't want to stop reading until you get right to the bottom of the sack!

'There are thirteen stories to a sackful and each and every one is a tried-and-tested cracker'
Sunday Telegraph

0 552 52730 0

CORGI BOOKS

A BASKETFUL OF STORIES
FOR SEVEN YEAR OLDS
Collected by Pat Thomson

Climb into this basket of stories and you will find . . . Charlie and his puppy, a wolf who tells riddles, a witch, a smelly giant, and many other strange and exciting people and animals. You won't want to stop reading until you get right to the bottom of the basket!

'Jam-packed with goodies'
The Sunday Telegraph

0 552 52729 7

CORGI BOOKS

A BUCKETFUL OF STORIES
FOR SIX YEAR OLDS
Collected by Pat Thomson

Dip into this bucketful of stories and you
will find . . . a ghost who lives in a
cupboard, a dog that saves a ship, a king
who can turn things into gold, a dwarf who
becomes a cat, and many other strange and
exciting creatures. You won't want to stop
reading until you get right to the bottom of
the bucket!

0 552 52757 2

CORGI BOOKS

A BED FULL OF
NIGHT-TIME STORIES
Collected by Pat Thomson

Snuggle up in bed with these wonderful stories.

By the light of the full moon, travel on a
flying quilt, dance with twelve princesses, or
learn how to make a ghost disappear. Here
are tales wrapped in the magic and mystery
of night-time from such well-loved authors
as Joan Aiken, Helen Cresswell, Dick
King-Smith and Philippa Pearce.

**'Pat Thomson's story collections are
always fresh, rich and entertaining.'**
Books for Keeps

0 552 52961 3

CORGI BOOKS

PHENOMENAL FUTURE STORIES
Collected by Tony Bradman

Who knows what the future will hold?

What do you think the world will be like in a hundred or a thousand years' time? The ideas in this superb collection range from the heavenly to the horrifying. Look into the future and discover . . . a boy cloned to provide body spares for his sporty brother; a bizarre city where the past is a secret and a talking ape fighting for his civil rights.

There are ten entirely original visions of the future here, from exciting authors including Lesley Howarth, Jan Mark and Julie Bertagna. Read these phenomenal stories and get a glimpse of the future.

From Tony Bradman, compiler of

Fantastic Space Stories
'A first-class collection'
School Librarian

Football Fever
'An excellent, easily affordable gift'
School Librarian

Sensational Cyber Stories
'Consistently of a very high quality'
School Librarian

0 552 54623 2

CORGI BOOKS

GRIPPING WAR STORIES
Collected by Tony Bradman

Tommy gripped the rifle in both hands and strained to listen as he crept through the Bosnian forest . . .

For Tommy war is only a game but for plenty of other young people it's a desperate fight for survival. Ahmed is sent to London as a refugee from sniper-scarred Sarajevo; Dafna is desperate for decent food when Jerusalem is besieged. Anton is caught up in a dangerous Resistance plot in occupied Amsterdam; and Younger Bear, a Cheyenne warrior, prepares for his first battle. The war zones are scattered across the globe but the excitement, the unpredictability and the terror of war touches them all.

Tony Bradman has collected ten inspiring stories of action, courage, fear and friendship in wartime which are sure to have you gripped to the very end.

0 552 54526 0

CORGI BOOKS

GOOD SPORTS!
A BAG OF SPORTS STORIES
Collected by Tony Bradman

Jump into this bag of sports stories and pull out hours of action-packed reading. Every one a winner!

Dive into the bag and meet . . . Dan, a talented swimmer who discovers an exhilirating new sport; Judith, who is determined to play in a tennis tournament; Sanjay and Mickey, who run into trouble when they are picked to play for the school cricket team; a group of girls who organize an unusual game of rounders . . . You won't want to stop reading until you get right to the bottom of the bag!

Ten never-before-published stories from a team of top children's authors including Robert Leeson, Michelle Magorian, Jan Mark, Anthony Masters and Jean Ure.

A CHILDREN'S BOOKS OF THE YEAR SELECTION

'A great read for sports-mad youngsters'
The Junior Bookshelf

0 552 54296 2
Now available from all good book shops

CORGI BOOKS

SENSATIONAL CYBER STORIES

Collected by Tony Bradman

*Boot up your imagination and log on to this
sensational collection of cyber stories.*

A bit of hacking for fun goes seriously
wrong when a rogue computer program
sends out the secret police to arrest the
school boy hackers; a boy swaps his brain
with his computer's memory, and amazes
all his friends with his command of facts and
figures; and virtual reality becomes blurred
in a thrilling but dangerous game . . .

Ten incredible stories involving state-of-the-
art technology and real human excitement
from top children's authors including
Malorie Blackman, Helen Dunmore and
Paul Stewart. Guaranteed to tempt even the
most addicted game-player away from the
computer screen!

0 552 54525 2

CORGI BOOKS

A BAND OF JOINING-IN STORIES
Collected by Pat Thomson

A great, action-packed collection of stories!

There are rhythms to clap along with, actions to copy, animal noises and repeated choruses as young listeners join in with a lion hunt, discover the Rajah's big secret — and even outwit a fearsome troll!

'Great fun' *School Librarian*

0 552 52815 3

CORGI BOOKS

**All Transworld titles are
available by post from:**

Bookpost
PO Box 29
Douglas
Isle Of Man IM99 1BQ

Tel : +44(0)1624 836000
Fax : +44(0)1624 837033
Internet http://www.bookpost.co.uk
or e-mail: bookshop@enterprise.net

Free postage and packing in the UK.
Overseas customers: allow £1 per book
(paperbacks) and £3 per book (hardbacks).